VLAD
THE WORLD'S
WORST
VAMPIRE

To Minkie, who is actually Malika and
– like Minxie in this book – is Very Good Fun
– A.W.

To my amazing friend, Amanda
(who may actually be related to Dracula)
– K.D.

First American Edition 2020
Kane Miller, A Division of EDC Publishing

First published in Great Britain in 2017 by STRIPES Publishing,
an imprint of the Little Tiger Group.
Text copyright © Anna Wilson, 2017
Illustrations copyright © Kathryn Durst, 2017
The moral rights of the author and illustrator have been asserted.

For information contact:
Kane Miller, A Division of EDC Publishing
PO Box 470663
Tulsa, OK 74147-0663
www.kanemiller.com
www.edcpub.com
www.usbornebooksandmore.com

Library of Congress Control Number: 2019956275

Printed and bound in the United States of America
2 3 4 5 6 7 8 9 10
ISBN: 978-1-68464-163-5

VLAD
THE WORLD'S
WORST
VAMPIRE

ANNA WILSON

ILLUSTRATED BY

KATHRYN DURST

Kane Miller
A DIVISION OF EDC PUBLISHING

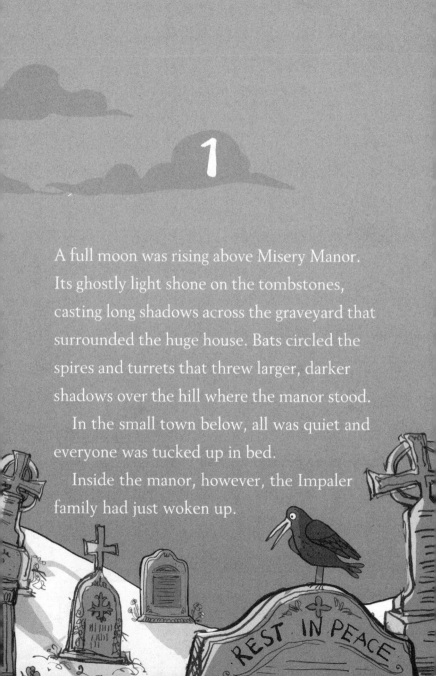

1

A full moon was rising above Misery Manor. Its ghostly light shone on the tombstones, casting long shadows across the graveyard that surrounded the huge house. Bats circled the spires and turrets that threw larger, darker shadows over the hill where the manor stood.

In the small town below, all was quiet and everyone was tucked up in bed.

Inside the manor, however, the Impaler family had just woken up.

One by one, they took their seats in the gloomy dining room at the grand oak table where they always started the night. The only light in the room came from a large chandelier that hung low over the table and was covered in cobwebs. A draft whistled in through the door and the old wooden beams creaked and groaned.

Countess Mortemia Impaler sat at one

end of the long table and Count Drax
Impaler sat at the other. Grandpa Gory,
the oldest member of the family, sat beside
Drax. Once they were settled, Mulch, the
butler, brought in the family's breakfast.

"Good morning," he said in his deep voice.
He put a tall glass of dark-red liquid in front
of each vampire and placed a fourth at an
empty space opposite Grandpa Gory.

"Thank you, Mulch," Drax said. "And my newspaper?"

"Here, Your Evilness," said Mulch, taking a copy of the *Vampire Times* from under his arm. He bowed low. "Will that be all?"

"Yes, yes. Off you go, Mulch," said Mortemia, waving at him impatiently.

After the butler had gone, Drax started reading the newspaper, and Grandpa Gory took a slurp of his breakfast and began leafing through a large book, peering closely at the pages.

Mortemia was the first to break the silence. She rapped her long red nails on the table and snapped, "For badness' sake! I can't stand this a moment longer."

Drax did not even look up from his newspaper. "Hmmm?" he said.

Mortemia tossed her long black hair over her shoulder. "Where is Vlad? You can be sure he

has overslept *again*! I promise I shall lock him in the Black Tower if he keeps this up."

Drax put down his paper and picked at his fangs lazily. "Good idea," he drawled.

"I often wonder if he really *is* your son," said Grandpa Gory. "He is so unlike you both. I sometimes think he has human blood in him. Mwhahahaha!"

Drax gave a slow smile and raised his glass of blood. "Ah, well, we all have a bit of that in us, don't we, Grandpa?" he said. "Mwhahahaha!"

"Oh, mwhahahaha! That's a good one, Drax!" Grandpa Gory laughed.

Mortemia bared her fangs. "There is *nothing* funny about suggesting our son is a human!" she cried.

Grandpa Gory muttered something under his breath and pretended to doze off, while Drax went back to his newspaper.

Mortemia grabbed a pepper shaker and slid it down the long table so that it hit Drax on the arm.

"Ouch!" Drax complained. "What was that for?"

"I need you to pay attention," Mortemia said with a snarl. "Vlad is failing in all his lessons. You should be putting aside time to help me teach him instead of flitting off to Transylvania whenever the mood takes you."

Drax frowned. "Can't this wait until later?" he asked. "I would like to have my breakfast in peace. Besides, I don't travel for fun – someone has to bring home the blood money."

Mortemia's eyes flashed. "Someone has to teach Vlad, too … and I don't see why it should always be me! I am going to give him his report this morning and I want you to be here when I do. Oh, where *is* he?" she

howled. "I blame Gory," she added between gritted fangs. "Vlad spends far too much time with the old fool."

Grandpa Gory opened one eye and, checking that Mortemia could not see him, he stuck his tongue out at her. Then he quickly shut his eye again and was soon fast asleep for real, snoring loudly.

"That's it!" Mortemia said, smacking her hands down on the table and waking Gory. "Mulch, go and get Vlad!"

She turned to look for the family butler and a figure stepped out of the shadows.

"Oh!" Mortemia cried. "There you are, Vlad. You gave me a fright."

"You should be pleased," said Vlad, under his breath. "You're always saying I'm not scary enough."

A little bat flitted around his head. "Oooh! Scary Vlad!" it squeaked in bat language.

"Do NOT talk to your mother like that,
Vlad!" Drax roared.

"That bat should be up in the belfry with
all the others," Mortemia said.

"Quite right," Drax agreed. He picked
up his glass to drain the last drops of blood.
"We've told you a thousand times, Vlad,"
he added, dabbing at his mouth with a large
white napkin.

"But Flit is my pet!" Vlad protested.

"Vampires do not have pets!" cried Mortemia and Drax in unison.

"Ah well, that's not strictly true," said Grandpa Gory. "If you had read the excellent *Encyclopedia of Curious Creatures*, you would know that our ancestor Count Marcovia Impaler kept six werewolves. They used to sit with him at dinner every night—"

"Do be quiet, Gory," snapped Mortemia. "Vlad – sit down. I am going to run through your report."

"You're in trouble now!" said Flit nervously, as he fluttered up to the safety of the chandelier.

Here we go again, Vlad thought, as Mortemia brought a scroll of parchment out of the sleeve of her dress.

He sat down and watched as his mother unrolled the parchment and began to read.

"Bat-morphing skills – E minus," she said with a sneer. "Everyone knows that vampires learn to fly as soon as they can walk. Not *you*, it seems."

"Sorry, Mother," said Vlad sadly.

"Evil laugh – E minus," Mortemia continued. "You sound like a twinkling star."

Drax let out a sigh. "If you can't fly or laugh like a vampire, there is no hope for you," he said.

Forget flying, Vlad thought, *I'd like to be able to make myself invisible right now.*

"And your academic work is even worse!" his mother went on. "You are a disgrace to the vampire race. Vampire history – F minus. Vampire folklore – F minus. Transylvanian grammar – E minus. Vampire math—"

"Enough!" Drax cried, rising from his chair. "What have you got to say for yourself, Vlad?"

Vlad shook his head. "I don't ... I don't know," he whispered.

"What about that excellent horror story I gave you? Have you finished it yet?" Drax asked.

"No," Vlad admitted. "It gave me daymares."

"DAYmares?" Mortemia screeched. "From a traditional tale of blood, guts and gore? *Blood Red and the Seven Bats*," she sighed. "How I loved that story when I was your age."

What, you mean two hundred years ago? Vlad thought. But he didn't dare say it out loud.

"So what *are* you reading?" asked Drax.

"Erm, nothing really…" Vlad said, crossing his fingers behind his back.

He thought of the book he had found one night while he was exploring the old library in the West Wing of Misery Manor. It had been tucked between the pages of a huge book on mythical beasts. *Jollywood Academy – the Best School in the World!* it

was called. Vlad couldn't stop reading it. He had stayed up to finish it, which was why he had been late for breakfast. And then he had needed to hide the book carefully. His parents would be furious if they discovered he had been reading a book about the human world.

"Well, this is very bad news," said Drax. He stroked his pointy chin. "You need to start some intensive flying practice. I will be checking on you regularly, young devil. I can see I am going to have to take you in hand, now that I am home."

"Surely you mean you are going to take him *under your wing*?" said Grandpa Gory. "Mwhahahaha! Get it? Flying lessons – under your wing?" He winked at Vlad.

"Hehehe!" squeaked Flit from the chandelier. "Under your wing! That's a good one."

"Silence!" Mortemia shouted. "I agree with your father, Vlad. As soon as you have had your breakfast, you must practice your flying. Now, drink up." She nodded toward the glass in front of Vlad. "We pay a fortune for Red Cells Express to deliver to our door."

"In *my* day," Grandpa Gory said, "we got our blood in the traditional way: by creeping up behind an unsuspecting human and sinking our fangs—"

"That will do, Grandpa!" Mortemia said.

Vlad made a face. He didn't care if the blood came from a sterilized bottle, delivered by a clean white van. He would much rather have a taste of one of those wonderful-sounding drinks the humans had in *Jollywood Academy*: hot chocolate or a slurp of strawberry milkshake or fizzy lemon pop through a twirly pink straw...

"Hurry up!" said Mortemia. "It will make you big, strong and handsome, like your father."

Drax flashed his pointy white fangs at his wife in what he clearly thought was a dashingly attractive manner.

Vlad drank the red liquid in one go and

18

tried not to make a face. He was vaguely aware of his father and mother telling him how they expected him to improve but he had stopped listening.

Instead he was nightdreaming that he was a human child at Jollywood Academy, the best school in the world! He thought of the pictures of happy human families dropping off their children at school. They all had colorful clothes and shiny hair – there was not a single pointy fang or black cloak in sight. The children had lots of friends and were always smiling. Vlad wished his life was like that.

Perhaps I could run away, he thought. He gazed out at the silvery moon. If only he weren't afraid of the dark, he could slip out into the graveyard and hide. But the thought of all those shadows and night noises made him shiver.

"You're not listening, are you?" his mother roared. "Right, that's it! Go to your room and clean your fangs!"

"Yes," Drax said. "And if you can't change into a bat by the end of the night, you will be locked in the Black Tower."

"Not the Black Tower!" Vlad whispered.

"That's a bit tough—" Grandpa Gory began.

"GET OUT!" Vlad's parents shouted.

Vlad turned and ran out of the dining room, with Flit flying close behind.

2

Back in his bedroom, Vlad flopped into his coffin and put his head in his hands. "I'm too tired to try to fly," he said in a muffled voice. "I want to stay in my coffin."

Flit was flying around him in little circles. "Cheer up, Vlad," he said.

Vlad looked up, his mouth quivering as a large tear rolled down his face. "It's all very well for you to say 'cheer up,'" he said in bat language. "You're already a bat! I'm never going to get the hang of my transformations," he finished with a sob.

Flit landed on the coffin next to Vlad. "You can't give up that easily," he said. "Remember how brave you were when you rescued me from that owl?"

Vlad sniffed and wiped his nose on his cloak. "I wasn't brave. I shouted because the owl had flown into my room and I was frightened."

"Well, you managed to scare off the owl and make it drop me!" said Flit. "I wouldn't have lived to tell the tale if it hadn't been for you." Flit hopped down beside Vlad and looked up at him with his beady black eyes. "And you're very good at speaking bat, so technically you're halfway there! Cheer up – for me?"

Vlad tried a small smile.

"That's better," Flit said. "Now, seeing as we're stuck in here, how about I help you with your bat-morphing?"

Vlad groaned. "I'm hopeless! And I'm covered in bumps and bruises from the last time."

"Going out in the dark is a lot less frightening if you're a bat," Flit said. "We bats aren't frightened of anything!"

"Except owls," Vlad reminded him.

Flit shook his wings. "True … but I was a baby then. Come on, try jumping off your

wardrobe. You can put some blankets on the floor to make a soft landing. Flying is fun! And it's much quicker than walking."

"I suppose…" Vlad said. "Although I can go fast on my skateboard." He whipped it out from behind his coffin. He'd seen a picture of a skateboard in his *Jollywood Academy* book and had decided to copy it. He had used a plank of wood and some little wheels that he'd found in Mulch's tool cupboard. He had painted the skateboard with beautiful swirls and stars until it looked almost as good as the one in the picture.

"I love my skateboard!" Vlad cried as he zoomed up a ramp – he had made that, too, from a floorboard propped onto a chair. "Wheee!" he shouted, as he flipped the skateboard up against a large wooden chest.

His bedroom was so huge that there was plenty of space for zipping around on the

board. And because his room was in the East Wing, away from the rest of the house, he could make as much noise as he liked. He mostly used it in the day, when he knew the rest of his family were in their coffins. It was no wonder he fell asleep in his lessons sometimes.

"It's nice to see you smiling," said Flit, watching Vlad perform flips and twists. "But what if Drax comes to watch you practice your flying? I think you should put that away now."

Vlad came to a sudden stop and flicked up his board with his foot to catch hold of the end. "Do I have to?" he said, his face falling.

"Come on, Vlad," Flit pleaded. "Try a bit of flying. I don't want to have to visit you in the Black Tower."

Vlad knew Flit was right. He dragged some blankets over to the wardrobe and piled them up so they were soft and squidgy. Then he pushed a chair against the side of the wardrobe. He climbed onto the chair and then, taking a deep breath, hoisted himself up onto the top of the wardrobe.

Flit flew up and hovered next to Vlad. "I'll be right here!" he squeaked. "Don't worry."

Vlad nodded and tried to feel brave. He opened his velvet cape wide, like a pair of wings. He closed his eyes and thought hard about flying like a bat.

"Ready…" said Flit.

Vlad gulped.

"Set…" said Flit.

Vlad shook his head. "No, I don't think—"

"GO!" cried Flit, giving Vlad a little push.

"Sooooooo!" finished Vlad as he teetered on the edge of the wardrobe and plummeted to the floor, missing the pile of blankets completely.

"Ouch!" he said, rubbing his knees.

"You need to get more lift under your cape," said Flit, swooping down beside him. "And you MUST concentrate on becoming a bat. You need to move, breathe and *think* like a bat if you want to become one."

"That's just it," said Vlad, exasperated. "I don't think I *do* want to!"

"Charming!" Flit squeaked.

"Sorry, Flit," said Vlad, softening. "It's just that yesterday – when I was reading *Jollywood Academy* – I thought that being human seems a lot more fun. I hate being a vampire! I don't like drinking blood and I don't like sleeping in a coffin and I'm afraid of the dark and all these cobwebs make me feel ill and … I HATE having no one to play with."

"Play?" said Flit, looking puzzled. "But you're a *vampire*. You're not supposed to play."

Vlad hobbled over to the window and saw

a familiar figure tottering unsteadily between the tombstones. Vlad watched Grandpa Gory walk up and down the rows.

"I wonder if Grandpa ever feels lonely," Vlad said. "There are no vampires *his* age around here either."

"Exactly how old *is* he?" Flit asked.

Vlad grabbed hold of the edge of his coffin as though it were Grandpa's walking stick and bent over. Then he said, in his best impersonation of his grandfather's voice, "Four hundred and two at the last count. Got a good couple of centuries left in me yet."

Flit squeaked with delight. "I love it when you do that! Do Mulch!"

Vlad grinned, then he let his face fall into a gloomy expression and he said in a deep, somber voice, "You called, Master?"

They both collapsed into fits of giggles.

"That's better," Flit said. He swooped and

dived above Vlad's head, turning somersaults and loop-the-loops.

But Vlad wasn't so easily distracted from his thoughts. *I'm only nine*, he thought. *That's a lot of years of being a vampire ahead of me. What if I never learn to do what vampires are meant to do?*

"Maybe if I had some vampire friends, I wouldn't be so useless," he said aloud.

"What makes you think that?" Flit asked.

"In *Jollywood Academy* the children have so much fun together. The school is near the sea," he said, his eyes lighting up. "They go on 'school trips.' They go swimming and have something called 'forest school' where they cook food over a fire. They eat yummy stuff called 'sausages' and 'marshmallows.'" Vlad sighed and looked sad again. "Even if I had a vampire friend, I couldn't do things like that."

"You have to forget about *Jollywood Academy*," Flit said. "It's making you sad.

You'll end up in the Black Tower if you don't show your father you can fly."

"I know," said Vlad. "Which is why I have to run away."

"WHAT?" said Flit. "Where would you go?"

"I don't know," said Vlad. "But I'll start by going down into the town. If real humans are as lovely as they are in *Jollywood Academy*, I should be able to make friends with them easily. Then they'll help me."

"That'll never work!" said Flit. "And anyway, humans sleep at night. No one'll be awake to help you."

"Which is why I'm going to go in the day," said Vlad.

"NO!" cried Flit. "You'll be burnt to a frazzle by the sun!" He leaped into the air and began flying around in anxious circles. "Remember the three most important rules of Vampire Health and Safety?" he said.

"I know, I know," said Vlad. Holding up a finger and, doing his best impression of his mother, he said, "The Vampire Health and Safety Code is: No Sun, No Sun and No Sun!" Vlad made a face. "And 'No Fun' either, if you ask me," he added. "Which is why I'm not going to give another hoot about it. I can cover up, can't I?" he added, pulling his cape around himself to demonstrate.

"Vlad—" Flit began.

"You won't change my mind!" Vlad said. "I don't even care if my skin *does* get burnt."

"Don't say that!" said Flit. "I care!"

Vlad's grim expression melted. "Thank you, Flit," he said. "But I'm still going."

"All right," said Flit. "Then I'm coming with you and we'll do it my way."

"Which is how?" said Vlad.

Flit flew upside down, grinning. "Listen – I have a brilliant idea!"

3

Vlad and Flit spent hours talking through Flit's plan. They argued over the details but eventually they had everything sorted out. The night was giving way to dawn when Vlad heard footsteps making their way along the creaky landing to the East Wing.

"Quick!" said Flit. "It's Drax."

"I hope this works," Vlad whispered. "I know Father gets dizzy easily ... but will it be enough?"

"It's too late now – he's coming! Hide!"

Vlad crept over to the suit of armor in the

corner of his room and hid inside while Flit whizzed around the dark and dusty rafters.

"Vlad?" Drax called, pushing open the door. "Have you been practicing? I want to see you turn into a bat."

"Wheeeeee!" cried Flit, zooming down from the ceiling at top speed. "I've done it! I've done it!" he squeaked as he flew in tight circles around Drax's head.

"What's that? Slow down, I can't see you properly!" Drax shouted, swatting his hands at Flit. "Is that really you, Vlad?"

"Yes!" shouted Flit, flying faster and faster. "It's really me! I've morphed into a bat! Are you proud of me, Father?"

Drax was spinning around, trying to get a good look at the bat. "I – yes, very good," he said, his voice becoming faint. "Slow down! You're making me dizzy!" he cried.

"That's just the problem," Flit squeaked,

making his voice sound panicky. "I don't think I *can* slow down!"

"Well … you'll … just have to TRY!" Drax gasped.

Suddenly the dizziness got the better of him and he fell to the ground in a heap.

"Quick!" Flit whispered, flying over to the suit of armor. "Let's go before he comes around!"

Vlad pushed open the suit of armor and stared at his father lying on the floor. "Is he going to be all right?" he whispered.

"He just fainted, that's all. He'll be fine. Come on – follow me!" said Flit.

Vlad tiptoed to his coffin, where he had stashed his skateboard, ready for a quick getaway.

"Don't forget your inhaler, Master Impaler!" Flit giggled softly.

Vlad grabbed his inhaler and his skateboard, and headed for the door.

The floorboards creaked as Vlad made his way out of the room, down the long corridor and through the dusty house, but the house was always groaning, so he told himself not to be scared.

Flit flew ahead, using his incredible sense of hearing to listen out for Mortemia.

When they reached the hall, a chink of

light shone through the heavy velvet curtains
that covered the front door.

"This is our chance!" said Flit. "Let's go."

Vlad pulled the hood of his cape up over
his head and slowly lifted the latch on the
heavy front door. Sunlight rushed in through
the opening and Vlad flung an arm up over
his face to block the fierce rays.

"Wow!" he gasped, blinking. "It's really hard to see, Flit," he said.

The little bat hovered in front of his face. "You'll be OK as long as you keep your hood up – and don't look directly at the sun!"

Vlad did as Flit said, closing the door behind him as softly as he could. Then he pulled his hood down even farther, wrapped his cape around himself to protect his pale skin from the sunlight and followed the little bat through the graveyard.

"Be ready to duck behind a gravestone if anyone comes," Flit squeaked.

"All right," Vlad said. "I'm getting used to the sun already, you know. It actually looks quite pretty here in the daylight," he added, as he made his way between the tombstones. "Those are nice," he said, pointing to a patch of yellow and white flowers growing in the grass.

"Hurry up!" said Flit, fluttering along

beside him. "If someone looks out of the windows they'll see us. You know Grandpa doesn't sleep well these days."

Vlad thought again about Grandpa, walking around the graveyard at night. Did he miss all those cousins and uncles and aunts who still lived in Transylvania?

It would be much more fun to meet them than learn about all the boring dead relatives in my history lessons, he thought.

Vlad had once suggested a trip to visit the rest of the Impaler family. He'd never met them and he liked the idea of getting to know his Transylvanian cousins. But his mother had said she would be glad if she never saw any of Those People for the rest of her life – and that was the end of that.

His mother must really dislike them if she didn't want to see any of them for a good six hundred years.

Vlad followed Flit down the hill to the town, glancing around anxiously. As they reached the bottom of the hill, Vlad's nerves almost overwhelmed him. He tried to distract himself by remembering the best bits of *Jollywood Academy*.

Think about the games they play in the playground! he told himself. *And the stories the teacher tells them! If only I can find a place like Jollywood Academy...*

"That would have been MUCH faster if you could fly," Flit sighed.

"For once in my life, I don't have to worry about flying. I can whizz along on my skateboard like a human now that we're on flatter ground. Watch!"

Vlad dropped his skateboard onto the pavement and hopped on, pushing off with one foot and zooming past a cluster of houses and shops.

As they approached the center of the town, Vlad spotted some children. He zipped behind a hedge and beckoned to Flit to hide with him.

"What are you doing now?" Flit asked.

"All the children are on their way to school – didn't you see?" Vlad said. "They must be – they're wearing the same sort of clothes as the children in *Jollywood Academy*. I want to follow them."

"OK…" said Flit. "But what if they see you? Humans hate vampires."

"I know that," Vlad said. "Mother has told me enough times." He put on his Mortemia voice again, saying, "'Vampires and humans are sworn enemies! We have hated each other since the beginning of time!'" He made a face. "She also goes on and on about something called 'garlic' that's poisonous to vampires."

Not that I'm a real vampire anyway, he added to himself.

He looked back up the hill at his home. It was so different from the lovely little houses down in the village, with their neat front yards. He turned back and peeked through the leaves in the hedge. More and more human families were walking past now – the children were chattering, laughing and running along in front of their parents.

"Come on, Flit. Let's follow them," said Vlad. He ducked out from behind the hedge

and sped after the children on his skateboard. Flit followed, then suddenly dived into the folds of his cape.

"Hey!" Vlad protested, stopping abruptly. "That's cheating!"

"Shhh," said Flit. "I'm hiding! Humans don't have bats as pets. And they don't speak bat language either. But don't worry," he added. "I'll stay with you the whole time."

"All right," said Vlad. He set off again, keeping his distance from the children but looking at where they went and how they behaved.

Some of the adults were walking with huge hounds on leashes. He knew from his reading that humans called them "dogs" and kept them as pets. He couldn't help feeling a little nervous. The hounds that vampires had were terrible beasts that chased you across the moors and gobbled you up.

Vlad stopped behind a large tree and watched as the children said goodbye to their parents and trailed in through the gates.

Inside the school grounds, children were running around, chasing balls and using a rope to jump over – all things that Vlad had read about. Someone had also drawn lots of numbers on the ground and children were hopping and jumping and turning on them in a rather complicated manner.

"They're playing!" Vlad whispered to Flit. "Do you think I could join in?"

"I think you should stop talking," Flit whispered.

Then all of a sudden something jabbed Vlad in the back, making him shriek in surprise.

"Why are you hiding behind a tree?" said a voice.

Vlad turned around slowly and found himself nose to nose with a small girl with curly black hair that was doing its best to explode from her ponytail in all directions.

"Maybe you don't understand English," the girl said. "Why – are – you – hiding – behind – a – tree?" She spoke very slowly.

"I was only looking," Vlad said, trying to sound brave. "What's wrong with that?"

"You were spying," the girl said. She folded her arms and narrowed her eyes. "You shouldn't do that, you know."

Vlad shook his head. "I wasn't," he said.

The girl put her hands on her hips and said, "Hmmmm." Then she seemed to take in his appearance for the first time. "Why are you dressed like that?" she asked. "It's not Dressing Up as a Book Character today. And vampires don't have those," she added, pointing at the skateboard. "What is it, anyway?"

Vlad felt a shiver of dread run through him. How did she know he was a vampire?

And weren't humans supposed to be frightened of vampires? But this girl didn't seem frightened at all. And what was the dressing-up thingummy she had just mentioned?

He decided it was best to say nothing.

"Never mind," she said, when he didn't reply. "But if you *are* going to dress up, you really should get the details right because you don't actually make a very convincing vampire." She sniffed. "You must be one of the new boys Miss Lemondrop told us about," the girl went on. "You'd better hurry up. We don't want to be late – Miss Lemondrop would KILL us." She drew her finger across her throat, made a strangled sound and rolled her eyes up into her head.

"No!" Vlad cried. "I'll make sure she doesn't do that!" Even vampires didn't kill people anymore.

"You're funny!" the girl said. "What's your name?"

"Vlad," said Vlad. At least this was one question he definitely knew the answer to.

"Weird," said the girl.

"Nice to meet you, Weird," said Vlad, holding out his hand.

The girl's face creased up with laughter again. "No!" she squeaked, "I meant your name *sounds* weird. My name's Minxie."

"Oh," said Vlad. He thought "Weird" was a better name but he didn't say so.

"It's short for Malika," said Minxie. "Sort of. I like it better than Malika anyway, so that's what I tell people to call me. 'Malika' means 'queen,'" she added, and made a face as though she was going to be sick. "And I am *definitely* not interested in being one of those. Think of all the pink and glitter I would have to wear. YUCK!"

Vlad didn't know what to say. He didn't feel very well prepared for this strange world of killer teachers and girls who laughed at him. It was not at all how his book had described human life.

"So how come you're changing schools in the middle of the year?" Minxie asked suddenly. "Where have you moved from?" She looked him up and down.

"I…" Vlad hesitated. "My family is from Transylvania," he blurted out.

"Wow," Minxie said, her eyes wide. She twisted her mouth into a thoughtful expression. "OK," she said, and grabbed his hand. "You'd better come with me. I'll look after you, don't worry."

Flit started squeaking softly inside Vlad's cape. "Something tells me that is exactly what you *should* be worried about!"

Vlad pulled his cape close. He had a

sneaking suspicion that Flit was right but he was too curious to let the little bat put him off.

This was his chance: he was going to human school!

5

As Minxie pulled Vlad toward the school building, a bell rang. It seemed to have a magical effect on the children – they stopped talking and shouting and playing, and ran to the front steps, where they arranged themselves into lines. The smallest children were in a line at one end of the playground and the tallest at the other.

Vlad wondered how on earth they knew which way to go. Luckily for him, he had Minxie to guide him.

"Stand behind me and do exactly what I

do," she said, before snapping her head to face the front as a tall lady dressed entirely in purple appeared on the steps.

The lady had an enormous pair of spectacles balanced on her nose but she didn't seem to know how to use them. One minute she was peering through them, the next minute she had taken them off and was looking around without them.

She squinted at the children standing in their lines and began walking up and down. When she got to Vlad, she stopped short and her face crinkled into a puzzled expression.

"Oh dear," she said, "someone has their days muddled up, don't they? Dressing up as our favorite book character is *next* week," she added. "Although you are a very convincing vampire. Well done."

"It's a good costume, isn't it!" Minxie agreed.

Vlad gulped. He looked around but
there was no way he could escape now,
surrounded by all these children. There
wasn't even any room to get his skateboard
on the ground for a quick getaway.

As if reading his mind, the teacher said, "I am afraid I'll have to put that – erm – contraption away in the bike shed." She took his skateboard from him. "As for your costume… Ah well, I can hardly send you home now." She tutted and shook her head. "Please tell your parents you have to come dressed up *next* week. And perhaps not as a vampire. Save that for Halloween, all right?" she said, smiling wearily. "Into class, please, everyone!" she called out.

"Which book character are you anyway?" Minxie whispered, as they filed into the building. "You can't be a cartoon character, you know. It has to be from a BOOK."

Vlad decided the only way he was going to get through the day was to try to act the part. He copied the way Minxie spoke to him, rolling his eyes. "I know *that*!" he said, trying to sound sure of himself. "Haven't you

ever heard of *Blood Red and the Seven Bats*?"

Minxie opened her mouth to reply but before she could utter a sound, there was a flurry of movement from inside Vlad's cape.

Vlad gasped in horror as he watched Flit fly in front of his face.

"What are you *doing*?" Vlad said, squeaking in bat language.

"What are YOU doing, more like?" Flit squeaked, flying up out of reach. "I didn't think you were really going to go into a human school!"

"Wow! A real live bat!" Minxie cried, pointing up at Flit.

It was Flit's turn to look horrified. He shot down the back of Vlad's cape but Minxie was still shouting and pointing.

"It's gone inside your costume, Vlad!" she said.

The other children had broken from their lines to see what Minxie was making such a fuss about – but Flit was now nowhere to be seen.

"What?" Vlad said. "No, there's nothing in my cape. Only me!" He pretended to be confident, even though his tummy felt as though a whole belfry of bats was whizzing around inside it.

The other children laughed.

"Everyone knows that bats don't come out

in the day," jeered a boy with short brown hair and freckles. "The only bat around here is YOU! Batty Minxie!" the boy laughed. "Completely bats, you are!"

"Oh be quiet, Boz," Minxie snapped. "What have you done with it?" she whispered to Vlad.

Vlad put on his best "innocent face" and shrugged. "I haven't done anything," he said.

"Goodness me, you are a chatterbox, Malika," said the purple lady with the enormous spectacles. "Come along. Classes are starting."

As their line moved down the corridor, Vlad opened his cape a tiny bit and whispered to Flit, "Stay in there and don't say a word!"

"You'll have to take that off," Minxie said, eyeing his cape.

Vlad felt fear grip his throat. He clutched the fabric closer to him and shook his head

57

vigorously. "I never take off my cape," he said.

Minxie frowned. "You really *are* weird," she said. "Come on, it's time for lessons."

"She's so bossy!" Vlad whispered to Flit. "I'm not sure I want to do lessons – I thought we would have more time to play."

"Too bad!" Flit squeaked. "If you walk out now, the teacher will want to know where you're going. She might even want to talk to your parents!"

But she won't be able to, Vlad thought. *They're fast asleep back at Misery Manor...* He forced himself not to think about home – or the trouble he'd be in if his parents ever found out where he'd gone.

Miss Lemondrop was standing at a desk at the front of the class.

"What's she doing?" Vlad whispered to Minxie, as he followed her into the room.

"She's getting ready to take attendance, of course – she's our teacher," said Minxie, turning and frowning at Vlad.

"Oh yes," said Vlad. He remembered that this was what the Jollywood Academy teachers did at the start of each day.

"You can sit next to me," Minxie said, grabbing Vlad's cape and leading him to an

empty desk. "And I think you should take your hood off now that we're inside," she added. "It looks weird."

Vlad hesitated.

"Go on," Flit whispered. "The sun can't burn you inside, remember?"

"OK," said Vlad.

He pushed his hood back slowly. The bright lights of the classroom made him blink but Flit was right. He didn't get burnt.

Vlad sat down next to Minxie and looked around at the other children. When the last child had come into the room, Miss Lemondrop looked up from her tidying and said loudly, "One … two … three!"

This seemed to have a similar magical effect as the bell ringing – all the children sat down, stopped talking and faced the front.

"Good morning, Badger Class!" the teacher said.

"Good morning, Miss Lemondrop," the class sang back in unison.

Badger Class? Vlad looked around the room. He had watched badgers playing in the graveyard and there definitely weren't any in here. Maybe they were allowed to play with the badgers after lessons.

Mind you, he was beginning to think that even the lessons might be fun. Miss Lemondrop didn't look like the sort of person who would get cross if he made a mistake.

I bet she wouldn't make me write out the names of Great-great-great Uncle Latvox and Great-great-great Aunt Bratislavonika's seventeen children, he thought. *And I bet she wouldn't send me to the basement to help Mulch polish every single piece of silver we own if I forgot one of the "greats."*

A person who allowed badgers into her class had to be a lot more fun than that, Vlad reasoned.

Miss Lemondrop had started taking attendance.

"Where are the badgers?" Vlad blurted out.

Miss Lemondrop looked up, frowning. "Who said that?" she asked.

"You dope!" Flit whispered from inside Vlad's cape. "You said that out loud!"

Vlad felt his mouth go dry as he saw that the whole class had turned to stare at him.

Suddenly the freckly boy called Boz burst out laughing. "He thinks there are *real* badgers in our class! What a weirdo!" he hooted.

Soon the whole class was whooping and giggling and pointing at Vlad.

Minxie wasn't laughing but she was watching Vlad very carefully.

Miss Lemondrop clapped her hands then said, "One ... two ... three," again and the children settled down. She peered at Vlad. "Are you sure you're in the right class? What's your name?"

Vlad opened his mouth to speak, but Minxie jumped in and said, "This is Vlad. He's from Transylvania."

"Oh!" said Miss Lemondrop, beaming. "You're one of the new children. How exciting! I had better explain – our class is just *called* Badger Class. Next door is Fox Class and the one down the corridor is Squirrel Class, you see?"

Vlad nodded. "Do you have a Bat Class?" he asked.

Boz burst out laughing again but Miss Lemondrop silenced him with a look. "No, dear," she said to Vlad, smiling again. "Did you have a Bat Class in your old school?"

If only you knew! Vlad thought.

"Er, yes," he said. "I was in, erm, Bat Class."

"Fascinating!" said Miss Lemondrop.

Vlad felt himself relax. "Yes, and this isn't a costume," Vlad said. He was getting into the swing of things now. "This is my national dress."

"What are you *doing?*" Flit squeaked quietly.

"Really?" said Miss Lemondrop. Her face shone.

Vlad ignored Flit. The teacher seemed to be really interested in what he had to say.

"Yes," he said, sitting up proudly. "In Transylvania the boys wear black suits, white

shirts, velvet capes and long black boots just like this, and the girls wear long black velvet dresses," he went on. "I thought I should dress smartly on my first day at school."

Minxie shot him a narrow-eyed look.

Uh-oh. Maybe I've said too much, Vlad thought.

"I see," said Miss Lemondrop. "Well, that's wonderful. And you certainly do look smart. However I think you'll have to take off your cape in class," she added.

Vlad hesitated.

"Come along," said Miss Lemondrop, holding out her hand. "I'll hang it up on the back of the door for now but in the future you must put it in the cloakroom. Malika can show you later."

"What about me?" Flit squeaked.

But Vlad just nodded at Miss Lemondrop and shrugged off his cape. He couldn't spend the whole day trying to keep Flit a

secret on top of everything else. Flit would
just have to hide inside the cape.

"That's better," said Miss Lemondrop.
"I can see your lovely suit now."

Vlad smiled back at the teacher. His
parents were wrong about humans being
nasty, he told himself. Minxie was being
kind to him and this teacher was lovely. If
they had been wrong about that, maybe they
were wrong about him getting burnt in the
sunlight, too?

As the teacher hung the cape on a hook on the door, Vlad heard Flit give a frightened squeak.

"What was that squeaking?" asked Miss Lemondrop, looking around the room.

"I-I think it was the door," said Vlad quickly.

"You must be right, Vlad," said Miss Lemondrop. She moved the door back and forth a few times.

Flit, thinking quickly, gave another squeak.

"Hmm," said Miss Lemondrop again. "I shall have to get the custodian to put some oil on those hinges."

While the teacher examined the door, Boz leaned over his desk and poked Vlad.

Vlad turned to see Boz sneering at him with an evil glint in his eye.

"Show us your teeth!" Boz said.

"W-why?" Vlad asked. He glanced at

Minxie but she said nothing.

"I saw them when you smiled," Boz said. "They're all pointy – like fangs!" He pulled back his lips and said in a spooky voice, "I'm a vampire!"

"Boz, stop being gross," said Minxie, although she frowned at Vlad.

But Boz got up from his seat and began pretending to be a monster. Vlad felt a surge of panic. Did this boy really know what he was?

Miss Lemondrop whirled around. "Sit down, Boswell Jones!" she shouted.

Boz dropped back into his seat with a scowl.

"What do you think you're doing?" Miss Lemondrop asked.

"Miss, he was being rude about Vlad's teeth," said Minxie. "Because they're pointy."

Vlad tried to make himself as small as possible.

"Don't be rude, Boswell. Now, Vlad," Miss

Lemondrop said, turning back to Vlad. "Smart as your national costume is, I should explain that here we have school uniforms, which we expect *everyone* to wear," she said kindly.

She gestured to the other children, who were all wearing blue T-shirts and black shorts or skirts.

"Perhaps we can get you something from the lost and found... Now, let's go over our times tables. And when we've finished, I think Vlad should tell us all about life in Transylvania. I am sure everyone has lots of questions."

He heard Boz snigger behind him. "Yeah, Freaky Teeth!"

Vlad froze. He couldn't talk about Transylvania... He'd never been there! How was he going to get out of this?

Vlad was surprised by how easy he found the times tables, compared to the tricky problems his mother made him do.

"You've done a very good job, Vlad!" said Miss Lemondrop, when he answered all the questions correctly. "The Transylvanians seem to be a bit ahead of some of us," she said, glaring pointedly at Boz, who had not been able to give any of the right answers. "That reminds me," she went on, glancing at the clock on the wall, "why don't you come up to the front and tell us about your home

country, Vlad?"

Vlad felt his mouth go dry. "I-I don't know," he said.

"Come on, dear," said Miss Lemondrop. "I don't bite!"

Vlad started. "I should hope not!" he blurted out. "In any case, your teeth don't look sharp enough."

"Yours do, though," said Boz, as the rest of the class sniggered.

"Boswell!" said Miss Lemondrop sternly. "One more word from you and I'll send you to the office!"

"Sorry, Miss," he mumbled.

From the look on Boz's face, Vlad thought that the office sounded as bad as the Black Tower!

Miss Lemondrop turned back to Vlad. "It would be lovely to hear about your home in Transylvania, Vlad," she said.

"Go on, Vlad!" said Minxie. "We want to know EVERYTHING about you."

Vlad looked around. Everyone except Boz was smiling and waiting to hear what he had to say. Back at home no one was interested apart from Flit!

Vlad steadied his nerves, pushed back his chair and walked to the front. He tried to remember everything his father and grandfather had told him about Transylvania. Clearing his throat, he started talking.

"My family comes from Transylvania..." He trailed off. What could he say, without telling them he was a vampire?

"Carry on, dear," said Miss Lemondrop, looking at Vlad and smiling.

"Yes, carry on, Vlad," said Minxie.

"They, umm... It's a big family," said Vlad. "There's my Auntie Pavlova and Uncle Maximus."

"Weird names!" Boz muttered.

Vlad frowned. There had been a boy called Jack in the *Jollywood Academy* story who was a bit like Boz. He was always being mean and playing pranks on the other children. Feeling cross with Boz seemed to have the magical effect of making Vlad feel brave again. He drew himself up tall.

"My family – the Impaler Family – is one of the oldest families in the whole of Transylvania!" he said, fixing his eyes on Boz. "We go back generations and generations. And we live in a big manor house – I mean ... we did ... in Transylvania," he added.

"Liar," Boz said quietly.

"Be quiet!" hissed Minxie, glaring at Boz.

"Fascinating!" said Miss Lemondrop. "And do you speak Transylvanian?" she asked. "Is that what the language is called?"

"Yes," said Vlad.

"Perhaps you could say something for us, then?" Miss Lemondrop said.

Vlad gulped. He was terrible at Transylvanian!

"Well, there wouldn't be much point, would there?" he said, thinking fast. "You wouldn't be able to understand it!"

The class laughed, which made Vlad bolder still. "I could tell you some Transylvanian jokes," he offered.

"Yes, please!" everyone shouted – except Boz, who was sulking.

Vlad thought of some of Grandpa Gory's favorites. "Why does Count Dracula have no friends?" he asked.

"We don't know!" said the class.

"Because he's a pain in the neck!" said Vlad.

The children all laughed and even Miss Lemondrop chuckled.

"What's Count Dracula's favorite sport?"

"We don't know!" shouted the class.

"*Bat*-minton!" said Vlad.

The laughter grew louder still.

Miss Lemondrop stood up at the front of the class and cried out, "One … two … three!"

Everyone settled down.

"Vlad, dear," she said, "that is very entertaining … but I was hoping you might tell us a bit about your life. What is school

like in Transylvania, for example?"

"Erm… It's a lot like it is here," Vlad said. "We have classrooms and teachers, and we do lessons about Transylvanian things," he said.

He saw that the class was starting to fidget and he couldn't think of anything interesting to say. "But – but I haven't been to school for a while. Since we moved I've been having my lessons at home." *It's easier to talk about what's true*, he thought. "My mother has been teaching me history and my grandpa teaches me Transylvanian myths and legends. He has a big book of them. He also has a book about mermaids and unicorns, but everyone knows they don't exist!" Vlad said with a weak laugh.

"How do *you* know?" Minxie piped up. "Just because you haven't seen one, doesn't mean they don't exist."

76

"Very good, Malika," said Miss Lemondrop, although she said it as though what she really meant was, "Be quiet, Malika." Then she turned back to Vlad. "What about your customs? And food... Do you have a favorite national dish?"

Vlad felt his stomach fall away. *I can't tell her that we drink blood*, he thought. Then he remembered the descriptions of the food the pupils had in their forest-school classes in the *Jollywood Academy* book.

"We have picnics in the forest sometimes!" he said. "With sausages cooked over a fire. And marshmallows," he added. "I LOVE marshmallows."

Miss Lemondrop looked rather puzzled. "How nice!" she said, with a small frown. "But presumably you have real meals as well – are your parents good cooks?"

"Oh no, we have a butler who does all

that," said Vlad.

"Oooooh! A butler?" Boz muttered. "How posh!"

Vlad didn't understand. He started babbling to cover up his confusion. "Er, he's called Mulch and he's very tall. When Father calls him to the dining room he comes in like this…" Vlad drew himself up tall and dipped his head in an impersonation of Mulch. Then he said in a deep, booming voice, "You called, Master?"

The children laughed again, so Vlad went on. "My grandpa lives with us. He's very good at telling stories but he's also good at falling asleep halfway through them. Like this…" Vlad sat down in Miss Lemondrop's chair and said in a quavering old voice, "When I was young, back in the olden days we often—" Then he pretended to fall asleep and let out an enormous snore!

OOAAOIIINNGNKK!

At that point, the bell rang and Miss Lemondrop had to shout over the noise.

"Break time!" she called. "Thank you, Vlad," she said as the children ran out to the playground. "You certainly have a talent for bringing a story to life!"

"My cape!" cried Vlad, as Minxie grabbed him by the hand and dragged him out after the others.

"You don't need it – look! It's a lovely sunny day," she said.

"I know," Vlad said, sounding panicky. "That's what I am worried about."

Minxie stopped. "What?" she said.

"I – er … I have an allergy," Vlad said, thinking quickly.

"An allergy to the sun?" said Minxie. Her eyes widened. "Really?"

"Yes – I might get burnt," Vlad whispered, looking around to make sure no one else had heard. Would Minxie suspect something?

But she just nodded and said, "Of course! You've got really pale skin. Don't worry, we can stay in the shade. Or I could go and ask for a hat and some sunscreen for you?"

Vlad didn't know what sunscreen was. He glanced at the back of his hands to check his skin. Nothing had happened – he wasn't burnt. Maybe his parents had been wrong?

"No, no, it's OK. I don't want to make a fuss," he said. "Let's just stay in the shade."

"OK!" said Minxie. "But lots of people with pale skin worry about the sun, you know. Not just Transylvanians." She looked at him a bit oddly when she said this, but then she added, "You were amazing in class just now! So *funny*!"

"Really?" said Vlad. No one had ever said

things like that to him before – not even
Grandpa Gory.

Minxie was jumping and twirling. "YES!"
she shouted, punching the air. "FUNNY
AND AMAZING!"

Vlad grinned.

"Hey, you know what?" Minxie said,
hanging from the jungle gym and pointing at
Vlad. "I've just had the most BRILLIANT
idea! You should audition for the school
show. You're dead good!" she said.

"Dead?" Vlad repeated, looking puzzled.
"Zombies are dead – except they're also
kind of alive. At least, that's what Grandpa
says."

Minxie laughed. "Your grandpa sounds
awesome. I can't believe you used to live in a
castle! And you have a butler – no one has a
BUTLER anymore! Are you rich? Can I come
to your house?"

Vlad's grin faded. "Er, oh, we don't have a butler anymore," he said, crossing his fingers behind his back. "Not since we moved from Transylvania. We don't have any money or a manor house anymore, either," he said.

Minxie jumped down, looking sad. "Aww," she said. "I'm sorry. Are you a refugee?"

Vlad bit his lip. "I-I don't know," he said. "I don't know what a refugee is."

Minxie smiled. "It's what we call people

who have had to leave their home to find a better place to live – because they feel unsafe, for example," she said. Then she put her arm through Vlad's and drew him in close. "Don't worry," she said, "I'll look after you. I know what it's like leaving all your friends and family behind."

"Do you?" said Vlad. "Why, what happened to you?"

"I'll tell you another day," Minxie said quickly. Then she said, "Are you lonely?"

"Yes," said Vlad, relief flooding his voice.

Minxie leaned in closer. "Shall I tell you a secret? So am I. Sometimes," she whispered.

Vlad thought Minxie seemed far too confident to be lonely. She was dancing around again, full of beans.

"Come on, let's get a snack," she said. "You can be my New Best Friend," she

added, skipping ahead to where a teacher was handing out fruit.

She wants me to be her best friend! Vlad thought. It sounded like the nicest thing in the world – someone to talk to, someone to stick up for you when things were tough, someone to have fun with!

All of a sudden it seemed as though nothing was impossible...

Minxie passed Vlad some segments of orange and an apple.

"Erm, do these have garlic in them?" he asked, remembering what his mother had told him about human food.

"GARLIC?" Minxie roared with laughter. "Don't you have oranges and apples in Transylva— Wait a minute, why is garlic a problem?" she asked, giving him one of her narrow-eyed looks again.

"Oh, it's only – I'm allergic," he said.

"You have a lot of allergies," Minxie said.

"Yes," said Vlad, and he whisked his inhaler out of his pocket and waved it in the air. "This is for my dust allergy and I have to stay out of the sun, and I absolutely mustn't eat garlic," he said.

Minxie seemed convinced. "Oh yes. Lots of kids have those," she said. "OK, I'd better go and tell the cafeteria people about the garlic – you're supposed to get your parents to write in about allergies, though," she added. "You'd better bring a note tomorrow. Anyway, wait here! I won't be long."

As Minxie ran back into school, Vlad let out his breath. *So far, so good*, he thought as he sank his tiny fangs into the mouthwatering apple and closed his eyes. He almost groaned aloud at how delicious it was. This was turning into the best day of his life!

A voice interrupted his thoughts. "There's

something not right about you."

Vlad opened his eyes to see Boz leaning toward him, just a bit too close.

"There's your teeth, for a start. You need to go to the dentist to get them fixed, you know," Boz was saying. "And why are you wearing that black suit?" Boz asked, poking Vlad in the chest. "It's freaky. You look like a waiter in a posh restaurant," he said.

Vlad looked around, gripped with panic. Every time he relaxed, even for a second, it looked as though he was about to be found out! Where was Minxie?

"I bet your Transylvanian school was full of posh weirdo boys like you," Boz said.

Vlad backed away from Boz. *Say something*, he told himself.

"Oh yeah, I forgot," Boz sneered. "You've been having lessons with your batty old grandad who reads you stories about

mermaids and unicorns." Boz let out a nasty laugh.

"Boswell Jones, that is ENOUGH!" said a teacher. He was looming over them and speaking in a booming voice that reminded Vlad of Mulch.

"Sorry, Mr. Bendigo," said Boz sullenly.

"I should think so," said Mr. Bendigo. Then in a much kinder voice he looked at Vlad and said, "You must be the new boy. Miss Lemondrop asked me to bring you these." He handed Vlad a small pile of carefully folded clothes with a pair of old sneakers balanced on top.

"Thank you, sir," said Vlad.

Mr. Bendigo looked very pleased. "How polite!" he said. "Now why don't you go and put on the uniform? The locker rooms are just over there, next to the bike shed." He pointed to the far corner of the

playground. "As for you, Boswell," he added, making his voice boom again, "you can go on trash duty."

Boz shot Vlad a look of fury and stomped away. Vlad let out a long sigh and looked around for Minxie. Why wasn't she back yet?

"There you are!" said a familiar voice from above him.

Vlad looked up and saw Flit perched on the wall!

"What are you doing?" Vlad whispered. He looked around hastily to see if anyone else had noticed.

"What are YOU doing, more like!" squeaked the bat. "You need to get out of here. That boy Boz is bad news."

"I know. What am I going to do, Flit?" he said.

"Leave," said Flit firmly. "Now."

"But what will Minxie think? And what about my cape – and my skateboard!" Vlad protested.

"It's too dangerous to stay, Vlad!" said the

little bat. "Remember how horrible humans can be. What if everyone finds out what you really are? Who knows what will happen to you!"

"But…" Vlad stopped. Maybe Flit was right. Vlad thought again about the character called Jack in *Jollywood Academy* – he had made life very nasty indeed for some of the other children. And what if Boz found out he was really a vampire? What would he do then?

"All right," Vlad said miserably.

"Good. I'll hide in your jacket – there's no time to go and fetch your cape. We'll have to stick to the shade," said Flit.

Vlad was looking around himself wildly. "Flit, how am I going to get out of here without being seen?" he said.

"I'll think of something," said Flit as he dived into Vlad's sleeve.

"Hey, that tickles!" Vlad protested. He nearly dropped the uniform he was still clutching.

"Shhh!" said Flit. "Start moving toward the gates – stick to the shadows and no one will notice."

Vlad wasn't convinced but he did as the little bat suggested, sticking to the wall that ran along the edge of the playground. He hugged the uniform to himself and made his way toward the school gates. He had almost reached it when a voice rang out across the playground. "Hey, where are you going?"

Vlad turned to see Minxie running toward him. "I've told them about the garlic allergy, so it'll be OK at lunchtime. Oh good, you've got a uniform! Can I have a turn on that board thing of yours now? I could get it for you. Puh-leeeese!" she pleaded.

Vlad didn't know what to do. How was

he going to get away from Minxie? Then he thought of something Boz had said about getting his teeth fixed.

"I have to go. To … to the den—" *What was it called?* "The – the dentist!" he said, remembering just in time.

"Really? Now?" Minxie said. Then she looked at him closely. "Hmm," she said. "Maybe your teeth are growing a bit too fast. But don't worry!" she said. "Dentists can do amazing things. My big brother had the wonkiest teeth you've ever seen. He got one of those metal things put in his mouth and now his teeth are as straight as lampposts."

Vlad took a few steps toward the gates. "Can you tell the teacher, please? I forgot to say. You can even have a turn on my skateboard."

"It's not a skateboard!" Minxie said, laughing.

"It is!" Vlad said, looking hurt.

Minxie was biting her lip, trying to stop her laughter. "It's a bit wobbly looking. Is it homemade?" she said.

"Actually," said Vlad, drawing himself up tall like Drax, "it's an original Transylvanian model that has been in the family for generations. And it goes faster than the speed of bat."

"All right," she said. "I'll test it out while you're at the dentist and see how fast it really is."

Vlad breathed a sigh of relief. Minxie was already running off to fetch the skateboard. Now was his chance to escape! No one was watching him – they had all gone back to their games.

But just as Vlad turned to make a run for the gates, he heard a booming voice say, "Where are you going, young man?"

Vlad stopped in his tracks. Mr. Bendigo was coming over to him.

"I need to go to the dentist," Vlad said, shaking in his boots. "I was going to get changed on the way," he added, holding up the uniform Mr. Bendigo had given him earlier.

The teacher was peering at Vlad's face. "Hmmm. Have you got a note? And where are your parents?" he asked, looking over the top of Vlad's head at the entrance to the school. "I should have a word with them."

Vlad's blood ran cold.

"I'll divert him!" Flit squeaked, zooming out of Vlad's sleeve. He flew into Mr. Bendigo's face, flapping his wings.

"Argh! What's that?" cried the teacher, swatting at Flit. He spun around and around, his arms flailing.

"Run, Vlad!" cried Flit.

95

Vlad ran, clutching the uniform that
Mr. Bendigo had given him. He didn't stop
running until he had reached the bottom of
the hill. He was so out of breath he had to
lean against a wall, wheezing. He pulled his
inhaler from his pocket and closed his eyes
while he took a couple of puffs.

"Phew!" squeaked a little voice in his ear. "That's the fastest I've flown in my life."

"Thanks for distracting the teacher like that," Vlad wheezed.

"That's all right," said Flit. "At least you're safe now."

Vlad glanced up at Misery Manor. "Am I?" he said. "I've got to face the music back there, haven't I? And I'm going to be in so much trouble for losing my cape!"

"Don't worry – we can think up an excuse," said Flit. "Come on. We need to get home."

"I'm going back to school tomorrow, you know," Vlad said.

Flit shot up into the air, flapping his wings and shrieking, "You must be JOKING!"

"Listen, Flit. Boz is just a bully and everyone else was really kind – much nicer than my family is. And the food was

delicious," Vlad went on. "And, even more importantly, look –" He held out his hands – "I haven't been burnt and I've been in and out of the sun ever since I ran out of school. You know what I think, Flit?"

Flit landed on Vlad's shoulder. "No. But I have a feeling I'm not going to like it."

Vlad looked grim. "I don't think humans *are* dangerous and I don't think the sun frazzles us and I even bet I'm allowed to eat garlic." He turned to look Flit in the eye. "Let's go back home now so I can get some sleep before breakfast. But…" he added, "I'm going back to school tomorrow. I have a uniform. And a New Best Friend. And school is so much fun. So, you can't stop me!"

9

Vlad was wheezing even more when he reached the top of the hill. He stopped behind a gravestone to use his inhaler and looked up at the manor.

"I hope everyone will still be asleep," he whispered anxiously to Flit.

"I'll go ahead of you to make sure the coast is clear," said the bat and off he flew.

When Flit came back, Vlad crept up to the heavy oak front door. He twisted the big iron handle and pushed very slowly, being careful not to let it creak on its rusty old hinges.

Flit flew into the dark entrance hall first, then Vlad followed, closing the door softly. He crept quietly up the stairs, along the landing and away from where his family were sleeping. He jumped when he heard Grandpa let out an extra-loud snore as he tiptoed past his room! He barely dared to breathe as he sneaked along…

Finally he reached his room, closed the door, flung the school uniform under his big velvet armchair and flopped into his coffin fully clothed.

"Aren't you going to take off your boots?" Flit asked, fluttering around Vlad's face.

But Vlad was already fast asleep.

That afternoon Vlad dreamed of auditioning for the school show. He was on the stage, dressed in a colorful outfit, singing songs and

telling jokes. The audience loved him. Minxie was clapping and shouting his name. Mr. Bendigo was smiling and shouting his name as well. And there was Miss Lemondrop ... she was coming up on the stage to congratulate him. She put a hand on his shoulder and said...

"Vlad – Vladimir Impaler! Wake up! What are you doing, sleeping in your boots?"

Vlad jumped and sat up too quickly. He banged his head against Mortemia's nose, and she sprang to the other side of the room with a yelp and fell into his armchair.

"Sorry, Mother," Vlad said woozily.

As he came out of his deep sleep, he remembered where he had been during the day.

Fear gripped him as he spotted the school sweater sticking out from under the armchair his mother was sitting on.

He tried to catch Flit's attention but Flit was
still hanging upside down, half-asleep.

"What is THIS?" Mortemia asked.

"Er ... er..." Vlad racked his
brains. "It was a present
from Auntie Pavlova,"
he blurted out. "Father
brought it back from
his last trip. Didn't he
tell you?"

"Yes, that's right,"
Flit squeaked sleepily.

"What?" Mortemia shrieked. "I am going to
have a word with your father about these
ridiculous presents. When would you ever
wear something as bright as THIS? It is most
un-vampiric." She screwed the sweater up into
a ball. "*Just* the sort of thing that ridiculous
Pavlova would choose. I shall have Mulch
destroy it immediately."

"No!" Vlad cried, leaping up from his coffin.

Mortemia frowned.

"I-I mean, let me take it to Mulch," Vlad said. "You have enough to do, Mother," he added sweetly. "And you're right. When would I wear anything so ugly when I have my lovely black suit?"

Mortemia raised her eyebrows and pursed her bloodred lips. "Very well," she said. "It just so happens that I am extremely busy," she said. "Your father was taken ill last night and is still feeling a little strange. He says he saw you turn into a bat before his very eyes! Mwhahahaha! Personally, I think it is bat-lag from all that long-distance flying. I keep telling him not to go Over There so much." She tutted. "And I could do without having to come and wake *you* up, young vampire!" she added, her voice rising to a screech.

"You have overslept AGAIN! You'll have breakfast in your room and Grandpa Gory is going to give you your lessons today."

She got up and marched out of the room, muttering, "What did I do to deserve such a son? Blazing blood cells, he's as batty as his grandfather."

"Phew, that was close!" Flit squeaked.

Vlad nodded, his face even paler than usual.

A few minutes later, the bedroom door opened again and in tottered Grandpa, looking as though he was still half-asleep.

"So, my young devil, are you ready for your lessons?" he wheezed. "I've brought your breakfast," he said, waving a glass. "Can't have a young vampire starting the night on an empty stomach, can we?"

Then, breaking into a loud fit of coughing, Grandpa Gory dropped into the armchair, sending up clouds of dust that made Vlad

cough and splutter, too.

"Now, where were we…?" Grandpa said, opening a huge leather-bound book.

But Vlad was lost in thought. *It's all right for Flit. He can fly wherever he wants. And bats don't need friends. Lucky them.* "What's lucky about being a vampire?" He clapped his hand to his mouth as he realized he had spoken out loud.

Grandpa Gory's wrinkly forehead crinkled even more. "What did you say?" he barked.

Fortunately for Vlad, Grandpa Gory was hard of hearing, so Vlad raised his voice. "I said, 'Isn't it good that we're vampires?'"

Grandpa nodded. "Yes, very good," he said. But Vlad couldn't help noticing that Grandpa looked a bit sad. "Certainly vampires had a lot of fun in the good old days," he said, turning his attention to the dusty book of myths and legends.

Vlad butted in, hoping to divert Grandpa Gory from starting a boring lesson. "Tell me about the time you changed into a bat and went out in the thunderstorm!"

"Oh, badness me! That was a good night," said Grandpa, perking up. "Lots of loop-the-loops around lightning bolts." He drew a pattern in the air with his walking stick and chuckled, shouting, "Wheeeeee!"

"Sounds fun, Grandpa," Vlad said.

"Ah – that reminds me, young Vladimir, how are you getting on with *your* flying lessons?" Grandpa asked.

"Not very well," Vlad mumbled.

"Well, we can't have that," said Grandpa. "How old are you now? Fifty-six?"

"Nine," Vlad said, rolling his eyes.

"Only nine? In that case, you are the perfect age to learn – full of energy. I was turning into a bat and whizzing around the place by the time I was your age!" said Grandpa.

Vlad groaned.

"No time like the present, eh, Flit?" Grandpa Gory said.

Flit squeaked, "Yes, come on, Vlad. Then we can fly ANYWHERE we like."

Anywhere... Vlad pondered. "All right," he said. "But I'm not going out on the roof like we did last time."

"No, no, we'll have a little indoor practice session first," said Grandpa. "Up you get – up there." He pointed at the oak wardrobe where Vlad had practiced only the night before.

"All right," said Vlad with a sigh.

He had just climbed up to the top when Grandpa said, "Where is your cape? You can't fly without your cape."

Vlad froze. "I-I think I dropped it somewhere," he said.

Flit fluttered around nervously. "Could he use yours?" he squeaked.

Grandpa Gory got up creakily and shrugged off his cape, muttering, "Young vampires today. Don't look after their possessions." He passed it up to Vlad. "There you are. Now, look after it! That cape was my father's, you know. Been in the family for generations."

Vlad smiled shakily and took the dusty old cape. He put it on, tied the ribbons around his

108

throat and stood looking down at the floor.

"Now, you know what to do," Grandpa called up to him. "Think 'I am a bat,' open your cape wide and JUMP!"

As if that will work, Vlad thought. He did as his grandpa told him, however. *I am a bat, I am a bat*, he repeated to himself, over and over. Then he opened the cape as wide as he could. He stared hard at his coffin, full of soft silks and velvets that he hoped would break his fall.

Suddenly he realized he wasn't thinking about being a bat anymore – he was only thinking about how much it would hurt if he landed on the hard edge of the coffin.

"You have to jump while you're thinking, remember!" Grandpa called up. "I always think of what my bat instructor taught me—"

"I know, I know!" Vlad said wearily.

"Batwings, Air, Travel."

"That's right – B-A-T!" Grandpa chuckled. "Good, eh? You can't go wrong."

Not unless you're completely useless like me, thought Vlad.

He tried again.

I am a bat, I am a bat, I am a bat.

He opened the cape.

And he jumped!

But the minute he jumped, he stopped thinking about being a bat and thought about how he really wanted to go back to school to see Minxie and Miss Lemondrop. And then he thought about how he would much rather be in school with them than flying through the air in his dark bedroom in his horrible home with his boring family and—

SPLAT!

He landed face-first in his coffin, with the oversized cape covering his head.

Grandpa collapsed into a laughing fit that ended with him coughing and wheezing. "My poor little devil," he said, wiping tears from his eyes. "Perhaps my cape was too heavy… What are we going to do with you?"

Vlad pulled off the cape and threw it on the floor. "Leave me alone, that's what!" he said. "I've got better things to do than learn how to turn into a silly old bat."

"Hey!" Flit squeaked.

"Sorry, Flit, but it's true," Vlad said. "Now both of you go away and leave me alone."

Grandpa Gory looked at Flit and shrugged. "Let's go out, Flit," he said. "I haven't been flying with you for ages. We can do some loops and twirls around the turrets. The moon is beautiful tonight."

"Yipppeee!" Flit said. His shiny black eyes flashed at Vlad. "I do wish you could join us, Vlad…" he added as he and Grandpa left the room.

A tear rolled down Vlad's face. He forced himself to drink his breakfast, which was now cold and gloopier than ever. He set the empty glass down on the floor, then opened

up the oak chest and pulled out his copy
of *Jollywood Academy – the Best School in the
World!* Everything about the story made him
think again about his school adventure. He
remembered how kind the teachers had been
and how delicious the fruit had tasted.

He knew what he had to do. Putting the
book in the oak chest, hidden carefully under
spare blankets and clothes, he got back into
his coffin.

*I'm going back to school and I am going to stand
up to Boz*, he thought. *And this time, I'm going
alone.*

10

A few hours later, Vlad woke with his heart banging in his rib cage. No one had bothered him all night and now it was dawn again.

He was almost shaking with excitement as he pulled on his school uniform and the pair of old sneakers, and threw his velvet bedspread over the top instead of his cape.

Just in case someone sees me coming out of my room, he told himself.

Flit was still fast asleep, hanging upside down from the rafters.

Vlad crept down the dark corridor and up

to the front door. He paused to check that no one had seen him, then let himself out into the sunlight.

He ran all the way down the hill, holding his bedspread out like wings. He felt free! Knowing that he wouldn't be burnt to a frazzle made Vlad so happy, he realized he was enjoying the feel of the air on his skin. A light breeze caught the fabric and for a moment Vlad wondered if it might actually be fun to fly for real.

I'm not going to think about that today, he told himself. *I'm not going to worry about any of the vampire things that I can't do. I'm going to have fun with Minxie instead.*

At least it was easier to run downhill without having to carry his skateboard. He got to the bottom of the hill and hid the bedspread in a bush before running through the streets to the school. Vlad smiled to himself. His parents really did not know what they were missing, living in the dark all the time.

As Vlad got closer to the school, however, his happiness faded. The town was rather quiet… He began to feel worried.

Maybe today isn't a school day, he thought.

But Minxie had said, "See you tomorrow," he remembered, so he kept running until he reached the school gates. He got there just in time to see the last

children filing into their lessons.

I'm late! he thought.

He reached the classroom as the children were settling at their desks.

When Vlad came in, Minxie broke into a wide smile.

"Come and sit next to me again, Vlad!" she called out.

"Minxie's got a new boyfriend," Boz sang.

"Oh be quiet, Boz," said Minxie, turning on him. "Or I'll tie you up with a jump rope and push you into the sandbox."

Vlad grinned. Minxie was like the girls who stood up to Jack in *Jollywood Academy*.

I wonder if Minxie knows that book? Vlad thought. *I shall have to ask her.*

He didn't have time just then, however, as Miss Lemondrop had appeared at the front of the class and was clapping her hands.

"Class!" she said. "One … two … three!" Everyone quieted down. "That's better." She took attendance and smiled when she came to Vlad.

"Don't you look smart in your uniform!" she said.

Vlad grinned, even though he could hear Boz blowing a raspberry behind him.

"Malika told me about your trip to the dentist – I hope it was all right?" she added.

Vlad nodded.

"Good. I came to find you at break yesterday to make sure someone was coming to fetch you, but there was a fuss in the playground, which I had to help sort out," she said. "Anyway, I'm sure I'll meet one of your parents later today, won't I?" she said.

Vlad swallowed hard and nodded again.

"Right, let's get on with our work," said Miss Lemondrop, turning her attention back

to the rest of the class. "Today we are going to work on our history projects," she said. "I hope you have all done some research on your family trees?"

Family trees? Vlad thought, groaning inwardly. *Not here as well!*

"Now remember to make the family trees colorful and decorative, as they will be displayed in the auditorium for Parents' Evening," the teacher went on. "Take your places at the art tables, please."

As everyone settled down and got out their pencil cases, Miss Lemondrop came over to Vlad and Minxie's table.

"Malika, will you show Vlad what we've been doing?" she asked.

"Yes, Miss!" Minxie replied. "Here," she said to Vlad, "you can use my pencils."

Vlad picked up a red pencil and stared at it. It was a bit like the quill he was used to,

he thought – it had a pointed end at least.
He couldn't see an inkwell anywhere on the
desk, so he decided to watch what Minxie
did and copy her.

Everyone settled down to work.

All Vlad could hear was the scratching of
pencils on paper. The pencils turned out to
be much faster to use than quills. And they
worked on their own – without any ink!

He bent over his work, writing down everything he could remember from his lessons with Mortemia.

Miss Lemondrop began walking around the room.

"My goodness! How extraordinary!" she said when she came to Vlad. She picked up Vlad's paper and showed it to the class. "Vlad knows his family tree as far back as seven generations! This is incredible," she said, returning the piece of paper to Vlad. "And what beautiful handwriting you have. It is almost like the Gothic script you find in ancient manuscripts. How wonderful! Your mother has obviously been teaching you very well."

"Th-thank you, Miss," Vlad said.

Minxie looked over at him and frowned. "Don't be too much of a Goody Two-shoes," she warned him. "Or I might not want to be your New Best Friend after all."

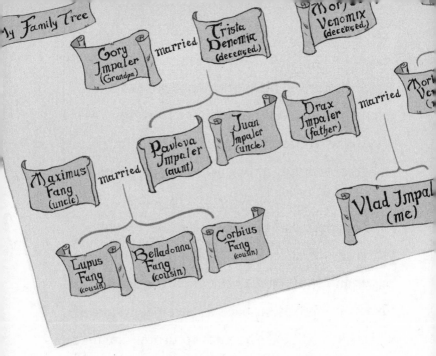

My Family Tree

Gory Impaler (Grandpa) — married — Trista Denomia (deceased)

Mor Venomix (deceased)

Maximus Fang (uncle) — married — Pavlova Impaler (aunt)

Juan Impaler (uncle)

Drax Impaler (father) — married — Mort Ve

Lupus Fang (cousin)

Belladonna Fang (cousin)

Corbius Fang (cousin)

Vlad Impal (me)

Vlad gulped and went back to his work.

Then something hit him. He felt with his hand and found a sticky ball of paper stuck to his back. He turned around to see Boz smirking at him. "The dentist didn't sort out your freaky teeth, then," Boz said. "Still pointy and weird."

"I have to go back for another appointment," Vlad said. He faced the front and did his best to ignore Boz.

"You didn't really go to the dentist, did you?" Minxie whispered.

Vlad's throat went dry. "I-I did," he said.

"The dentist is near the station," Minxie said, "but you went the other way. Where did you go? And why didn't you come back after lunch?"

Vlad couldn't speak. He bent his head over his work and pretended to concentrate on his family tree.

"You're going to have to tell me if you want to be my best friend," Minxie persisted. "Can I come over to play at your house after school today?"

Vlad gulped. "Maybe," he whispered. "I-I'll have to ask my mother."

"Great," she said.

Vlad closed his eyes and tried to breathe normally.

Oh, Flit, he thought. *What am I going to do?*

At break time, Vlad rushed outside ahead of all the others. He wanted to find a quiet corner where he could sit and think but Minxie caught up with him too quickly.

"Here – you forgot your snack," she said, handing him half an orange. "When you've eaten it, let's get out your funny skateboard!" she said.

"OK," said Vlad. Perhaps that would stop her asking him any more awkward questions.

As soon as they had finished their juicy oranges, Minxie grabbed his hand and dragged him to the shed. She pulled out the board from behind a pile of bikes and scooters.

"Thanks for letting me use it yesterday, by the way," she said. "I tried to do some tricks but I don't really know how. I've never seen a

board like this before. Will you show me how it works?"

He dropped the board and hopped onto it, then did his best to impress her with a routine of jumps and flicks and turns that he had taught himself in his bedroom back at Misery Manor.

"Wow!" said Minxie. "How do you *do* that?"

"I'm not really sure," Vlad said. "I just kind of think about what I want to do and then do it."

Minxie laughed. "I think flying must be like that!" she said.

Vlad stared at her. How was it that she said things that were so close to what was really going on in Vlad's life?

"I guess you'll have to teach me some tricks when I come over to play," Minxie said, breaking into his thoughts. "Where *do* you live? You still haven't told me. Because I know you said you had moved here. *Obviously* you can't be coming from Transylvania every day!" Minxie giggled. "I mean, I don't know *exactly* where Transylvania is because we haven't done it yet in geography – although I bet we will now that you're Miss Lemondrop's new pet—"

"I am *not* a pet!" Vlad blurted out. "I'm a va—" He gasped and stopped himself. "I mean, I'm a *boy*, not a pet!" he said. He put

his hands on his hips and made himself sound extra indignant to cover up his nerves.

Minxie roared with laughter. "You are *funny*!" she said. "Sorry if that sounded mean," she said. "I guess you have a lot to learn. Don't worry, I'll help you out... As long as you tell me where you live, of course," she added.

Vlad opened and closed his mouth a few times, then said, "I live out of town, actually. That's why I was late. It ... it takes ages to get here."

"Yeah?" said Minxie. "WHERE outside town? You don't live in that big old manor house on Spooky Hill, do you?" She held up her hands and made "Whooooo" noises.

Vlad's pale face went whiter than ever.

Minxie exploded with laughter again. "I know you don't live *there*, silly! That house is HUGE. You'd have to be mega rich to live

there." Vlad nodded. "And mega spooky!" Minxie continued. "It looks like the kind of place *vampires* would live. And you're not a vampire, are you?" she asked, her eyes glinting in the sunlight.

And before poor Vlad could think of what to say to that, the bell rang.

11

Vlad managed to get through the rest of the day with no more difficult questions. He enjoyed a lesson called English where he got to write a story and draw pictures to go with it. He'd written about his flying lesson and gotten a gold star. Miss Lemondrop had told him it was the most imaginative story she had ever read!

In the afternoon, everyone had gone outside to play games with balls and hoops and small squashy beanbags, and there had been lots of running races.

By the end of the day, Vlad was exhausted.

Now I really do wish I could fly, he thought, as he saw Minxie coming up to him. *What am I going to do?*

"I-I need to get my cape from the classroom," said Vlad, thinking that would give him an opportunity to shake her off. "I left it here yesterday. And I should get my skateboard, too."

"OK. I'll come with you," Minxie said.

Vlad sighed. "Thanks," he said.

They went back to the classroom to fetch the cape, which Vlad put on, then they walked to the shed. As they went, Minxie kept up a running commentary about everything, from how annoying Boz was to how weird it was that Miss Lemondrop wore so much purple to how tall Mr. Bendigo was. "I think he should be called 'Mr. Bend-so-low' because he has to

130

bend over to talk to us!" she giggled. "What do you think, Vlad?"

"Hmm?" said Vlad. He was still trying to work out how he was going to get away from Minxie. As though she was reading his mind, she linked her arm through his so he had no chance of escape!

"Which one is your mom?" Minxie was saying as they neared the crowd of grown-ups at the school gates.

"Oh ... she's not here yet," Vlad said. "What about yours?" he asked, trying to keep his voice casual.

"I get the school bus," Minxie said. "Mom works and Dad doesn't live with us anymore. The babysitter looks after my little brother and my big brother's in college."

Vlad thought Minxie looked a bit sad when she said this.

"But the good news is," she went on, "it

means I can come to your house and I don't have to ask for permission. I'll just tell the bus driver I have a playdate. Wait here!" she called over her shoulder as she scampered to the school bus.

Suddenly Vlad felt a hand on his shoulder. He looked up and saw Miss Lemondrop. "There you are, Vlad. I'm glad I caught you." She smiled. "Is your mom or dad here? I need to speak to them."

Vlad must have looked very anxious because Miss Lemondrop took off her glasses and said, "No need to worry. It's nothing bad. You have a lot of talent! I hope you'll be auditioning for the school show later this year. But I must ask your parents to formally enroll you. I checked our lists and we don't seem to have the name 'Vlad Impaler' anywhere."

"I'll tell Mother she needs to see you," Vlad said. "But I'm going home with Minxie now. Sorry," he said. "She's waiting for me." His fingers were crossed again. He wondered how many fibs he had told in the past two days.

Miss Lemondrop beamed and said, "I'm so pleased you and Malika have made friends. She needs a friend like you. Have fun, Vlad. And see you tomorrow!"

In spite of his fears, Vlad felt himself

tingle with pleasure at her words.

"Goodbye, Miss!" he said.

He waited until the teacher had gone, checked that Minxie was still nowhere near, then hopped onto his skateboard. He was about to zoom off when he heard a familiar voice in his ear saying, "What do you think you're doing?"

Vlad whirled around to see Flit hovering by his head.

"What do you think *you're* doing?" Vlad squeaked. "Get inside my cape, quick!"

"Only if you come home," Flit said.

"Don't worry," Vlad said crossly. "I was just leaving anyway." He was grateful to see Flit but also angry that the little bat had been spying on him!

Vlad turned to go but in that instant, lots of things happened at once.

Flit zipped into Vlad's cape just as Minxie

134

began making her way across from the bus stop. She spotted Vlad and waved.

Vlad jumped onto his skateboard and pushed off as hard as he could, his cape billowing out behind him in the breeze.

"Wait for me!" Minxie shouted from the other end of the playground.

Vlad cried out, "I wish I could *fly* home!"

The wind caught Vlad's cape and—

POOF!

He was a bat!

"Whoopeee!" Flit shrieked, flying a loop-the-loop. "You did it!"

Minxie stopped in her tracks, looking all around, an expression of pure confusion on her face.

"Race you, Flit!" Vlad laughed.

They whizzed through the streets and up the hill, leaving Minxie and the school far behind.

When they got back to Misery Manor, the sun was still shining.

Thank badness, thought Vlad. *There'll be time for a snooze before breakfast.*

"You'll have to switch back now," said Flit when they reached the graveyard.

"OK!" said Vlad. "But how?"

"Think 'V-L-A-D,'" said Flit.

"What?" said Vlad. "That's my name."

"Ye-es," said Flit slowly. "So it should be easy for you to remember: Vampire – Land – Air – Down … VLAD! In other words, think about being a *Vampire*, pick a spot to *Land*, fly through the *Air* and go *Down*."

"All right," said Vlad. "Here goes…"

Vampire – Land – Air – Down, he thought.

He picked a spot in the graveyard where there were no tombstones and began flying

toward it, thinking *Vampire, Vampire, Vampire* all the way.

BONK!

He fell out of the air too soon and landed on top of an old gravestone.

"Ow!" he said.

"Shhh!" Flit warned.

Vlad looked up at the old manor house but it was as silent as the graves surrounding it. He tiptoed up toward the front door.

"Do you think I'll be able to turn into a bat again?" he whispered to Flit.

"Yes! You'll have to practice your landing, though," Flit sniggered.

"Wow," said a breathy voice. "That was so cool!"

Vlad whirled around to see Minxie, panting from her climb up the hill, carrying his skateboard. He froze. How was he going to get rid of her?

Flit dived back into Vlad's cape. "Get rid of her!" he squeaked. "Think of something – quick!"

But Vlad couldn't think at all.

"I *knew* you weren't telling the whole truth," Minxie said, a look of triumph on her face. "Are you actually a real, live vampire?"

"Vampire?" Vlad laughed. It sounded like a pretty fake laugh, even to him. "Me? Noooo! What a funny thing to say!" he babbled.

Minxie threw down the skateboard and crossed her arms tightly. "You're fibbing!" she cried. "I saw you just now – one minute you were a bat and the next you were YOU again. *And* your teeth look like mini fangs," she said, counting the evidence off on her fingers, "*and* you were worried about eating garlic *and* you told all those jokes about vampires. And you have a vampire cape," she finished, holding up five fingers as if this were all the proof she needed. "I know I'm right! So you had better tell me what's going on or I'll tell everyone at school your secret."

"They'd never believe you," said Vlad, his heart hammering in his chest.

Minxie gave him a look that made it quite clear she wasn't going to let him get away with this.

"Do something!" Flit hissed, trembling inside Vlad's cape.

But Vlad knew it was too late for that.

"You're right, Minxie," he said, his head drooping. "I'm a real, live vampire. And this –" he pointed to Misery Manor – "is my home."

"WOW!" said Minxie. "Can I come in?"

"No! If my family finds out I've brought a human here, they'll never let me go outside again. My family hates humans," he added sadly.

"Why?" Minxie asked. "What have humans ever done to vampires? It should be the other way around. After all, you SUCK OUR BLOOD, don't you?"

"NO!" Vlad said indignantly. "We don't. We ... we get blood delivered nowadays."

Minxie arched one eyebrow. "Seriously?" she said. "Prove it." And she started off in the direction of the front door of Misery Manor.

Vlad ran after her. "No, you can't go inside!"

"Stop her! Stop her!" Flit squeaked.

But it was too late. Minxie had pushed open the heavy oak front door and was walking in.

Vlad and Flit caught up with Minxie in the hallway.

Vlad grabbed her sleeve. "Seriously," he whispered. "You can't come in here. Mother will lock you in the Black Tower if she finds you!"

Minxie shook his hand off her and stuck her chin in the air. "I'm not frightened," she said.

Vlad knew by now that Minxie was the sort of person who always got what she wanted.

"All right," he said wearily. "But we have to tiptoe. If you wake up my parents you really *will* be in trouble."

"Whatever," Minxie said. Then, looking up and up at the tall vaulted ceiling, she said, "This. Is. So. COOL!"

"Shhh!" pleaded Vlad. "It's always cold here."

"No, silly," said Minxie. "I meant it's cool as in *fantastic, amazing, epic*."

Vlad stared at her blankly.

Minxie curled her lip. "Boy, do I have a lot to teach you."

Flit squeaked nervously. "Mulch might wake up soon!"

"Come on, let's go to my room," said Vlad. "It's in the East Wing – far away from my parents' room, so it'll be safer than hanging around down here."

Suddenly a spider fell from its web and

dangled on the end of a thread in front of Vlad's face. "ARGH!" he shouted.

But Minxie cupped the spider in her hands. "I LOVE spiders."

"Shhhh!" Vlad insisted. "You're making too much noise."

"You're the one who shouted," said Minxie.

Just as she said this, they heard a STOMP, STOMP, STOMP.

"Mulch!" whispered Vlad, his eyes wide in horror.

"What?" said Minxie.

"Quick!" said Vlad. "Hide!"

Vlad pushed Minxie behind one of the suits of armor.

"I'll distract him," said Flit. But he was too late. The huge, looming figure of Mulch appeared in the gloom, swatting Flit away. Poor Flit went cartwheeling through the air

145

and landed on top
of the chandelier,
squeaking miserably as
one of his wings was singed
by the candles.

"You called, Master Vlad?" said Mulch,
his large body casting a shadow over the
little vampire.

"Er – n-no," Vlad stammered. "I was just having one of my ... daymares again," he said. "It's those stories Father makes me read," he added. "They give me the horrors! I think I must have been sleepwalking."

"Sleepwalking outside, Master Vlad?" Mulch said slowly. "That is dangerous. You might get burnt by the sun."

Vlad froze. How did Mulch know he had been outside? Vlad pulled his cape close around himself. "Outside?" he said, trying to sound innocent. "Did I really? I've only just woken up, you see."

"I hope you didn't sleepwalk into any *humans*, Master Vlad," Mulch went on.

Vlad gulped. "Humans? No..."

Flit fluttered down from the chandelier and whispered, "Stop talking, Vlad! We need to get away from Mulch, not keep him chattering."

Mulch lifted his nose to the air and sniffed. "I'm sure I can smell humans, Master. Maybe I should bolt the door during the day. For your own safety," he added.

The bolts were so high, Vlad would never be able to reach them to let Minxie out! He struggled to keep the panic out of his voice. "No, it's all right, Mulch," he said. "Grandpa doesn't like the door bolted. You know what he's like... Flit will make sure I don't do it again. Won't you, Flit?" he said.

"Too right," muttered Flit.

"By the way, Master Vlad," Mulch went on, "here's your book." He handed Vlad his copy of *Jollywood Academy*. "I found it while I was cleaning in your room."

Vlad's voice came out in a squeak. "H-how did you know? Mulch, please don't tell—"

"Who would I tell?" said Mulch. "I don't think anyone around here would be interested."

He gave a slow, deliberate wink. "I, on the other hand, love a good story. And *that* –" he said – "is a *very* good story."

"You're a – a legend, Mulch!" said Vlad.

"So I have been told, Master Vlad," said Mulch, bowing low. "I should warn you though, Master," he continued, "you are going to have to be *very* careful if you ever 'sleepwalk' again. You know what those humans are like."

"Yes, Mulch," Vlad said.

Just then, there was a muffled giggle from behind the suit of armor.

Mulch raised his nose and sniffed the cold, damp air.

"There's nothing here!" Vlad blurted out.

Mulch shuffled over to the suit of armor. "It is my duty to protect you…"

Flit nipped at Vlad's cape. "Think B-A-T, Vlad! Quick!"

Vlad didn't stop to ask why. He put all his efforts into thinking Batwings – Air – Travel and *POOF!* he turned into a bat just as Flit whisked his cape from him.

Flit dropped the cape on top of Minxie and pulled up the hood to hide her face just before Mulch peered behind the suit of armor.

"Oh," said Mulch, looking confused. "It's you, Master Vlad. How did you move so fast?"

"I changed into a bat," said Minxie, doing a very good impression of Vlad's voice.

Mulch's somber face broke into a wide grin. "Congratulations, Master," he said. "Your parents will be so pleased." He gave a deep, throaty chuckle. "You'll be getting your Bat License in no time."

"Y-yes," said Minxie.

"Well, I am sure you must be very tired, Master," Mulch said. "I will leave you to go back to bed. Good day." He gave a deep bow and headed back to his parlor.

"Good day," said Minxie.

Vlad waited until Mulch had disappeared in the gloom, then he thought *Vampire – Land – Air – Down*, and landed with a thud on the floor. He picked himself up, feeling bruised but pleased.

"That was so cool!" Minxie whispered, her eyes wide. "My New Best Friend is an amazing vampire!"

Vlad grinned. "Maybe I'm not as useless as Mother and Father think," he said.

Minxie giggled. "No. But you definitely have the world's worst landing technique."

Flit laughed. "Yes, you'll have to work on that."

"I know," said Vlad. "Now that I have two best friends," he added, looking at Flit and Minxie, "I reckon I can do anything!"

And he threw back his head and gave a real vampire laugh: "Mwhahahahaha!"

Jollywood Academy

The Best School in the World!

It was the end-of-term party at the beach. The class had played games, swum in the sea and lit a campfire with the help of their teacher, Miss Burdock. She had cooked sausages for the children and they had gobbled them all up. Now the flames were dying and it was almost time to go home.

"I don't want today to be over," Millie protested. "Tomorrow it'll be the holidays, which means no more Jollywood for six whole weeks!"

Because Jollywood Academy was the best school in the world, no one ever wanted to go home.

Miss Burdock smiled. "The party's not over yet," she said. "You see those lovely hot embers that are still glowing?"

The children peered at the remains of the campfire. "Yes!" they chorused.

"They are PERFECT for making our

dessert," Miss Burdock said. Her eyes twinkled in the light from the setting sun. "And do you know what that is?"

"No!" chorused the children, their faces shining.

"MARSHMALLOWS!" cried Miss Burdock. Everyone cheered.

The teacher passed round long toasting forks and said, "And now I will give each of you a lovely squidgy marsh— Oh!" she exclaimed, as she searched the picnic baskets. "Where are the marshmallows?"

Suddenly a groan came from behind a rock.

"I recognize that voice," said Millie. She stomped over to the rock. "Jack Biggins!" she cried. "You've eaten them all – and now you're sick. No wonder!"

Anna Wilson LOVES stories. She has been a bookworm since she could first hold a book and always knew she wanted a job that involved writing or reading or both. She has written picture books, short stories, poems and young fiction series. Anna lives with her family in Bradford-on-Avon, Wiltshire, England.

www.annawilson.co.uk